It's Tootle Time!

Tootle Tales

To Tim, Tyler and
Sarah-Ashley
– M.C.

For Lee, Harrison and
Marshall
– P.S.

All trademarks are the property of
Tootle Time Publishing Company
Cade, LA 70519

tootletime.com

ISBN 0-9721706-0-X

Library of Congress Control Number 2002093304

Printed in Singapore

Book Design: Peri Poloni
Knockout Design, www.knockoutbooks.com

MR. TOOTLES

and Those Oodles
of Noodles

Written by **Maryceleste Clement**   Illustrated by **Paul Schexnayder**

One day not long away
but surely not **yesterday,**

there lived an odd fellow
who was so very **mellow.**

Mr. Tootles was his name –
a likeable fellow but very **strange**.

He was tall, kooky and lanky,
very friendly and never **cranky**.
Except...

One day it came to be
that Mr. Tootles could not **see**,
what the answer was to be
of a problem he discovered over **tea**.

Mr. Tootles always had tea at three;
      he always drank with Mrs. Bea.
She was a very dear friend indeed;
      so sweet and kind, she helped all in **need.**

Mrs. Bea wore a flowered hat
and always had a cat in her **lap.**

She looked to the left; she looked to the right.
She whispered to her cat,
"There's a real funny **sight!**"

"What are you doing, Mr. Tootles?"

"Well, Mrs. Bea, my tea has noodles."

"At a quarter past three, noodles in your tea?
Oh my, I think I now see!"

Oodles of noodles were growing
everywhere–

the steps, the chair
and even in their hair!

"**M**r. Tootles, Mr. Tootles,
you have a problem with **noodles!**

Now that I look, I think I can **see**
your noodle problem is **larger**
than a noodle problem should be!"

Mrs. Bea said
with her face
turning red,

"Mr. Tootles,
Mr. Tootles,
please stop
with your
doodles!

You must get rid of all of these noodles!"

"**N**oodles, noodles **everywhere!**
Oh stop Mr. Tootles! Don't you care?

P eople, people everywhere –
      everyone is stopping to **stare!"**

"**M**r. Tootles, my dear friend,
with your smirk and your **grin**,

noodles all over your **hair**
and golly you don't **even care!**"

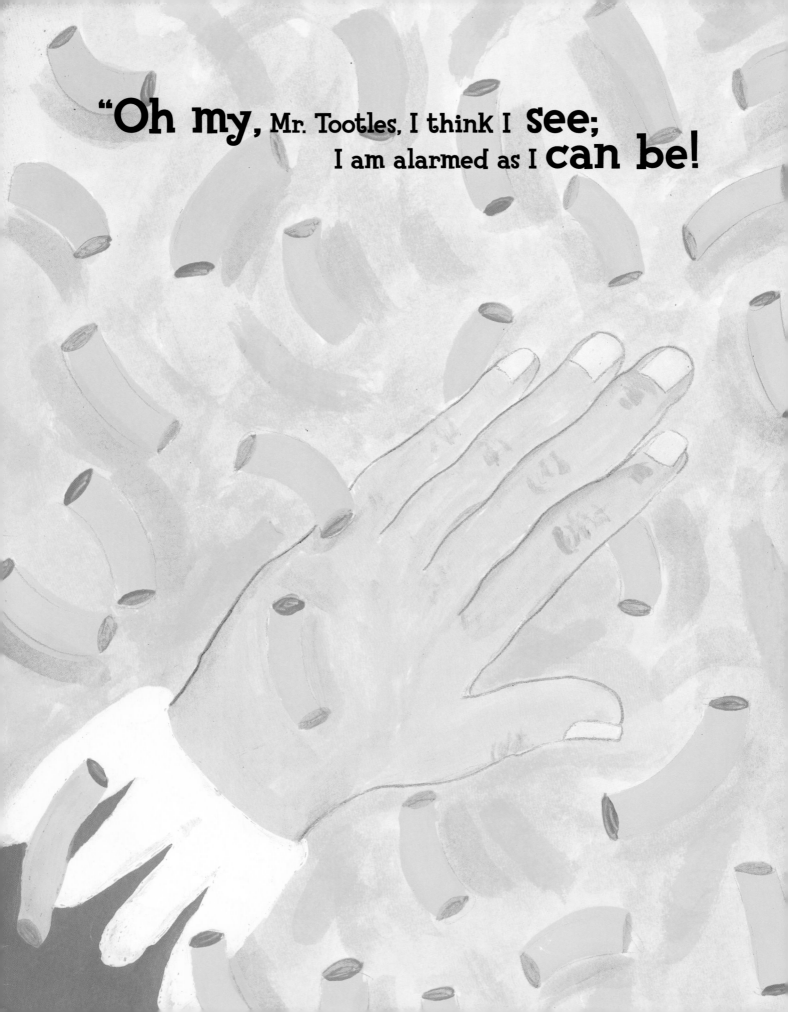

"**Oh my**, Mr. Tootles, I think I **see**;
I am alarmed as I **can be!**

Let me help fast as I can;
Let's do this **hand in hand.**"

"**M**r. Tootles, Mr. Tootles, please remain **calm.**
Close your eyes and sing a song,
a lovely sway to a sweet little tune.

And let's pretend it's a really **full moon!**"

"Now keep your eyes closed.
Clap you hands;
pinch your **toes**.

Look to the left;
look to the right.
Do not be afraid;
this will not cause a **fright**."

"Now, Mr. Tootles with all of your **noodles,**
I want you to think of my hot apple strudel.

Please be still; I need you to **focus.**

Get ready for some silly
hocus-pocus."

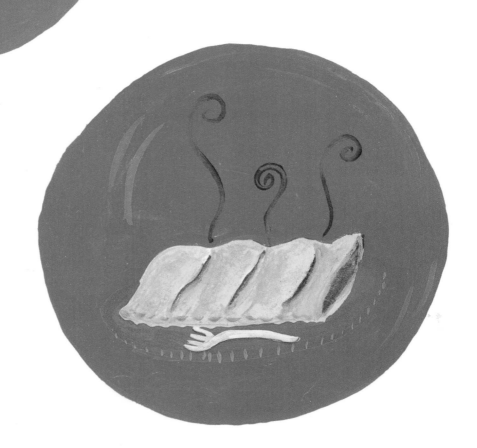

"My magic wand
    is circling your head."
Tap, Tap, Tap,
"You have nothing to dread.
    Now snap your fingers
        as quick as you can.

Please tell me now,

how ARE you my friend?"

Mr. Tootles slowly opened his eyes,
and turned to look up at the **skies.**

He looked to the left;
he looked to the right.

Then he saw such a
beautiful **sight.**

NO oodles
of **noodles.**

NO oodles
of **doodles.**

"**Look,** Mrs. Bea
and Kitty Cat!

Not even noodles in my **hat!**"

"**Oh my,** where did they all go?
Dear friend, thanks for helping me **so!**"

Mr. Tootles started jumping with glee.
"No noodles, no noodles! I am **set free!**"

"**Now** come here and have a seat next to me and I will pour you a nice **cup of tea.**"

Tootle-loo!

Tootle Tales

To order additional copies contact

TOOTLE TIME
Publishing Company

www.tootletime.com

Post Office Box 62
Cade, LA 70519

Printed in Singapore